For my children, whose creativity and curiosity fill my heart with endless inspiration. And for my dad, whose wisdom and impact continue to inspire me every day. This book is for you, and for every child who dares to dream big.

THE TINY TYCOONS
CyberMental

First published in Great Britain in 2025 by:
Grolightly Publishing
www.thetinytycoons.com

Paperback ISBN 978-1-0683957-0-3

Illustration and Book Design by:
www.happydesigner.co.uk

THE TINY TYCOONS

CyberMental

Written by
Dolapo Adeyemi

Illustrated by
Sarah-Leigh Wills

Chapters

Introduction

Hey there! I'm Max, and my sister Mia just spilled her super glittery, extra sticky glue on my favourite comic, "Rattle Bear." Ugh! But guess what? That disaster sparked something amazing. Welcome to Tycoon Town, the place where we, the Tiny Tycoons, transform everyday objects and wild ideas into real, exciting creations!

Mia's the artist in the family – she can turn a box of crayons into a masterpiece. Me? I'm the brains (shh, don't tell Mia I said that). I love puzzles, especially turning my wild ideas into cool gadgets.

In our world, there are two kinds of people: Creators, like us, who make epic stuff, and Users, who just chill and enjoy what's made. Creators are like undercover superheroes with a secret lab, making everything from robots to rocket ships. Users? They're the ones having a blast with all the cool things the Creators make.

But our adventures aren't just with crayons and glue. We've got a whole digital playground out there! It's like jumping into a video game, where we can build virtual castles, program our pets to do homework (still working on that), and create games that even make broccoli fun.

Guess what? You're officially invited to join our Tiny Tycoon crew. You've got the power to be a Creator – building, inventing, and maybe even causing a little (safe) chaos. But remember, being a Tiny Tycoon isn't just about having fun. We've got to use our brains, be smart online, and balance our screen time with real-world adventures. it's easy to just play and use what others have made. But there's a secret – when you create, you learn more, you grow more, and you become a star, shining bright in the world!

This book is your all-access pass to our world. We're going to share our top-secret tips on being awesome Creators, smart Users, and staying cool in the digital world. From crafting your first invention to mastering the art of not getting lost in the screen sauce, we've got you covered.

So, grab your favourite snack, find a comfy spot, and get ready to dive into our world of imagination, creation, and a bit of controlled chaos. Welcome to "Tiny Tycoons: CyberMental" – where your ideas light up brighter than a supercharged light bulb!

But what does 'CyberMental' mean? It's all about using your brain to create, share, and stay smart in the digital world. Think of it as a mix of 'cyber' (the digital playground) and 'mental' (your awesome brain power)!

Chapter 1: The Magic of Making (Becoming a Producer/Creator)

Update Patch #1: The Great Playground Makeover

Hey, it's Mia and Max here! Guess what? Our neighbourhood park is stuck in the Stone Age – seriously, it's like time forgot this place. Translation: It's old and boring. So, we decided it's time for "Operation Playground Makeover." That's right, we're turning from everyday park-goers to master creators, ready to give this old park a blast into the present!

Before we dive in, let's get one thing straight: what's a producer? No, not someone who makes movies (though that's cool too). In our world, a producer (or a Creator) is like a wizard with a toolbox. They take 'what ifs' and turn them into 'wow, look at that!' Producers / Creators are the ones who make stuff - from the comics we read to the games we obsess over.

So, Mia grabbed her rainbow markers and started doodling away. She dreamt up a playground that would make even unicorns jealous! *She imagined colourful murals, a treehouse with secret codes, and swings that played music. Her creativity was infectious, and soon, all the children in town were brainstorming ideas. Mia showed that creating or producing starts with a single creative spark.*

And Max? He turned into a puzzle-solving ninja. *He saw the playground revamp as a big puzzle, figuring out which materials to use, how to make the structures safe, and how to include something fun for everyone. Max's approach taught everyone that producing also involves problem-solving and thinking of others.* He figured out how we could use old tires for a climbing wall and empty soda bottles for a walkie-talkie system. Because, why not?

Fast forward through a montage of painting, hammering, and a minor glue incident (don't ask), and voila! Our playground started looking like the one in our heads. We weren't just playing in the park; we were creating our fun universe!

We didn't stop with swings and slides at the physical playground. Max put on his tech-wizard hat and coded a virtual version of our playground. It was like jumping into a video game – but one we made! Mia added treasure hunts and mystery quests because every playground needs a bit of mystery, right? With Max's coding magic turning our playground into a digital wonderland and Mia dreaming up stories and game plots, we discovered that making cool stuff isn't just about the stuff you can touch.

Did we mess up?
?
You bet.
We painted trees purple (turns out, it looked cool), and our first swing... well, it swung into a mud puddle.
But every oops moment got us closer to something awesome.

And then came our digital playground, bugs and all. Ever tangled with a digital bug? They're trickier than ants at a picnic, but every glitch taught us something new.

Being a creator (also called a producer) is like having a magic wand. Except instead of a wand, you have your brain (and sometimes loo roll – and glitter glue). It's all about turning ideas into real, amazing stuff. Stuff that makes you, and maybe even others, super happy.

- **For Artsy Wizards:** Love drawing or crafting? That's producing magic right there!

- **Tech Geniuses:** Into gadgets and games? Start with coding your own game or building a mini robot.

- **Story Magicians:** If you're all about stories, start penning down your own. Who knows, you might be the next big author or director!

- **Eco-Heroes:** If you have a green thumb, your garden is your canvas. Plant, nurture, and watch your creations grow!

Every idea is special—some big, some small. All have the potential to grow into something amazing if you give them a chance! Not every idea will work perfectly at first, but with each try, you'll learn and make your next idea even better.

SO, WHAT WILL YOU CREATE TODAY?!

Here's what you need in your producer toolkit:

- **Imagination:** It's your secret ingredient. Dream big, and then dream even bigger.

- **Curiosity:** Got questions? Good! Ask them, explore, and let your curiosity lead you to awesome places.

- **Never-Give-Up Attitude:** Sometimes, creating is tough. But remember, every mistake is a step towards something epic.

- **Teamwork:** Sharing ideas with friends or family can make creating even more fun.

Ready to start your journey? Create a 'Dream Board.' Stick pictures, drawings, or anything that inspires you. Put it somewhere you can see every day. It's your map to the treasure of creativity and it will remind you of your goals and dreams.

So, Tiny Tycoons, remember this: every time you create something, you're not just making stuff; you're making magic. You're learning, growing, and shining like the super cool creator that you are. Let's turn those 'what ifs' into 'no way, you made that?!'

At the end of our project, we and our friends looked at our new playground with pride. We had transformed our beloved space with our own hands and ideas. We were no longer just users of the playground; we were its creators. And in that moment, we understood the true magic of making – the joy of being creators.

Update Patch out,
Mia & Max (currently trying to get Max unstuck from the duct tape).

Dream
Board

Chapter 2: The Joy of Sharing (Value of Your Creations)

Update Patch #2: Sharing Our Creations

Max here, with Mia currently turning our living room into an art gallery (seriously, it's like a paint explosion). Anyway, let's talk about something super cool – sharing our creations! Because why keep all the awesomeness to ourselves, right?

Mia and Max's Share-a-thon

So, we built this epic new playground and a digital world (yep, we're pretty awesome like that), and then it hit us – let's share this coolness! Why? Because sharing is like levelling up in the game of creativity.

Mia went full Picasso and set up an art show in the park. Picture this: a sea of colours, crafts, and a bazillion paper cranes. People from all over town came, and the joy was contagious – like a laughter virus, but the good kind.

Inspired by Mia's art fest, I (Max, the cool one) hosted a storytelling hour at the library. I unveiled my interactive stories, and let me tell you, it was like a mind-blowing trip to Imagination Land. Kids' faces lit up, and I felt like a storytelling rockstar.

Oh, and get this – when the park got all litter-y, we jumped into action. We crafted these funky, colourful recycling bins and whipped up a game about saving the planet. Sharing our ideas, we turned Trashville into Clean City.

We didn't stop at the real world. We invited buddies to our digital playground for a virtual party. Watching them explore the digital world we created was like seeing our Brainchild take its first steps. Proud moment!

As more children in Tycoon Town saw what we had shared, they too were inspired to create and share. Soon, the town was buzzing with young creators, each adding their unique touch. Art, stories, games, and inventions were shared, making the town a vibrant hub of creativity and joy.

Sharing your creations is like sending them on a grand adventure. It's not just about showing off; it's about sparking ideas, smiles, and maybe even starting a creative revolution.

- **Inspiration Station:** Your cool robot or zany story might just light a creative spark in someone else.

- **Happy Multiplier:** Seeing others enjoy your stuff? It multiplies the happiness – like a happy math equation.

- **Feedback Fiesta:** Sharing means learning what rocks and what could be rockier in your creations. It's all about growing.

- **Friendship Factory:** Sharing brings people together. Who knows, you might meet your new bestie or sidekick.

Share-o-Meter: Where to Share

- **Home Base:** Family = your fan club. Show them what you've got!

- **School Showcase:** Your school is like a mini world – perfect for sharing your masterpieces.

- **Online, but Safe:** The internet is huge, so with a grown-up's guide, share your stuff in cool, kid-friendly corners.

Every time you share, you're giving the world a piece of your awesome imagination. It's like being Santa, but for cool ideas and fun stuff.

Mia & Max's Guide to Smart & Safe Digital Sharing

1: Choosing the Platform

2: Deciding What to Share

3: Privacy Check

4: Posting Online

5: Responding to Feedback

6: Sharing Success

7: Lesson Learned

Challenge Time!

Here's your mission, should you choose to accept it:

Create a story or comic and share it. Watch as your creation becomes a ticket to adventures for others!

STORY TITLE: ....

....

....

....

....

....

....

....

....

....

....

....

....

....

....

....

COMIC STRIP TIME!

Sharing: The Heart of Tiny Tycoons

Okay, so let's break it down! Sharing ideas is awesome because when we share, we get to work together and make our ideas even cooler. Plus, we get feedback that helps us tweak things and take our creations to the next level. And guess what? When we share, we inspire others to think big, too. It's like turning our ideas into something bigger, and we get to see the magic happen!

But, hey, sharing isn't always perfect. Sometimes, people might not get our idea, or their feedback could feel a little... harsh. And even if someone else claims your idea is theirs, or has a similar idea, remember—it's how you bring it to life that makes your idea truly unique!! That's why it's important to know when an idea is ready to be shared and when it needs a little more time.

Update Patch out,
Max & Mia (who's now trying to unstick her fingers from the glue gun – again).

Chapter 3: Wise Using (Being a Smart Consumer)

Update Patch #3: The Smart Consumer Quest

Max here, and Mia's busy comparing her five shades of blue paint. Yep, five! So, we've aced being creators, but guess what? We've got another mission: becoming super smart consumers. Sounds like secret agent stuff, right? Let's dive in!

Our first stop? The toy store. As we wandered the aisles, we noticed something: not everything was as awesome as it looked. Some toys were flashy but broke easily, while others were expensive but didn't do much more than the less-expensive ones. That's when we remembered: being a smart consumer means thinking carefully about what we buy. It's not about buying the coolest toy or the cheapest deal—it's about choosing what you really need and what will make you happy for more than just a day.

The Toy Store Dilemma

PICTURE THIS: Mia's eyes on this sparkly paint set (even though she's got a zillion at home), and me staring at a robot-building kit that costs as much as a small spaceship.

Mia's thinking, "Do I really need it?" After a quick battle in her mind, she decides to stick with her trusty paint collection. After all, wants are cool, but needs come first.

Needs vs. Wants - Mia's Decision

As for me? I picked the robot kit needed for my school project. While pricier, it felt like a smart choice. Sure, it's a bit more expensive, but it's top quality, packed with learning, and will last longer than my piggy bank's current balance!

Quality over Quantity - Max's Choice

Being a smart consumer doesn't just happen in stores—it's about making smart choices wherever we are, even online. During our digital escapades, we set a timer (because time flies when you're having fun online), picked games that gave our brains a workout, and double-checked for safe and sneaky-ad-free zones-because being a smart consumer also means protecting our time and making sure we're not wasting it on things that don't matter

- **Detective Mode On:** We turned into mini-detectives, researching before buying anything.

- **Eco-Heroes:** We also thought about Mother Earth, choosing eco-friendly stuff.

- **Saving for the Big Stuff:** Instead of spending on impulse, we started saving for things that really mattered.

We didn't keep these tricks to ourselves. Nope! We spread the word in Tycoon Town, turning everyone into wise consumers. It was like unlocking a new level in a game.

Remember, a Smart consumer is a mastermind of choices. Like a ninja, they cut through the clutter and focus on what truly matters. It's about making informed decisions that help you and the world around you.

0
5
10
15
20

- **Treasure Your Time:** Time's like gold; spend it on stuff that matters. We decided to play for an hour, keeping time for other activities.

- **Choose the Good Stuff:** Pick things that are safe, fun, and brain-boosting. We picked games that were fun but also taught us something new

- **Planet Protectors:** Making wise choices means you're also saving the planet. We started choosing products that were environmentally friendly. Go, eco-warriors!

What can children like Mia and Max do to protect the planet in their daily lives?

PLANET PROTECTORS

EVERY CHOICE COUNTS

Eco-warrior Challenge: Can you complete them all?

Tick them off as you go!

Recycling Day: Collect and recycle as much paper, plastic, and glass as you can find at home.

Water Wisdom: Keep track of all the times you turn off the tap while brushing your teeth.

Power Saver: Ensure all lights and electronics are off when leaving a room.

Green Thumb: Plant a seed or help take care of a plant.

Eco-Explorer: Go on a nature walk and make a list of all the different plants and animals you see.

Can you do all these in 1 week?

1. **Question Everything:** Do you need it? Is it safe? Is it useful? Ask away!

2. **Mix It Up:** Balance your day with digital fun, creative projects, and some good ol' outdoor action.

3. **Pause Before You Click:** In the digital jungle, think before you click or buy. We made sure the websites were safe and we didn't share personal information.

4. **Ad Alert:** Ads can be tricky. They try to get you to buy things you don't need. Learn to spot them and make your own choices.

5. **Save and Plan:** We decided to save our allowances for things we really wanted instead of buying on impulse.

6. **Research Before Buying:** Mia and Max learned to read reviews and ask for their parents' opinions before making a purchase.

Mia and Max shared their experience with friends, teaching them how to be smart consumers. They made a game out of finding the best value items and understanding the difference between needs and wants.

Scan the QR code to play >>>

Challenge Time! Plan Your Perfect Day

Here's a cool mission for you: Plan an awesome day that mixes up different activities. Show how you can rock being a balanced consumer of time, fun, and tech! Use the template at the end of this Update Patch.

As we close this chapter, remember, every choice you make as a consumer is powerful. It shapes your life and can even change the world in tiny, cool ways. So be curious, be smart, and choose like the awesome Tiny Tycoon you are!

Update patch complete,
Max & Mia (currently trying to rescue Mia's blue paint from our cat, Fluffy).

Awesome Day Planner

S M T W T F S DATE:__/__/__

Good Morning

Weather:

Today I will:.......................

....

....

7am:......................................

8am:......................................

9am:......................................

10am:......................................

11am:......................................

Good Afternoon

Daily Doodle:

12pm:......................................

1pm:......................................

2pm:......................................

3pm:......................................

4pm:......................................

5pm:......................................

Good Evening

How was your day?

Tomorrow I will:.......................

....

....

6pm:......................................

7pm:......................................

8pm:......................................

9pm:......................................

10pm:......................................

Check out the download available on our website!

Chapter 4: The Hidden Side of Free Things

(Understanding 'You as the Product')

Update Patch #4: The Mystery of 'Free' Stuff

After learning how to make smart choices with our money and time, Max and I realized something important: being a smart consumer isn't just about spending money. It's also about understanding why things are free.

So, we're playing these cool online games, right? Free apps, free games and free videos are awesome, but it got us thinking, "What's the catch?" Turns out, sometimes when things are free, YOU might be the product! Crazy, right?

Our buddy Ellie the Explorer (who knows everything about everything) dropped a knowledge bomb. In the digital world, when something's free, companies might be using our playtime or the information we share to make money for themselves, usually by bombarding us with ads.

Imagine this: every time you play a game, a sneaky ninja steals a little bit of your game time to build a big 'ad castle.' You wouldn't walk around with a 'For Sale' or 'Buy Me for Free' sign, right? So why give away your time and attention for free online? Before you know it, you're not just playing; you're spending your time building someone else's castle – for free! Funny, huh? But also makes you think – who's really winning the game here?

Ellie showed us these free games were like ad festivals. "Those ads are like digital billboards," she said. "Companies hope you'll see them and beg your parents for the latest super squishy slime or whatever."

And get this, some apps are like super nosy neighbours. They keep tabs on what we do in the game. Sure, it can make the game cooler, but sometimes they share that info with other companies who are super curious about what kids like us are into.

We realized our personal info is like our secret treasure. We don't want just anyone getting their hands on it. It's all about privacy, like keeping your diary locked away from your annoying little brother.

When personal information like your name, address, or even your birthday gets out there, it can be like giving a treasure map to internet pirates. They might pretend to be you to trick others or even buy things using your family's money without anyone knowing. Keeping your information safe helps make sure no one can play tricks or take things that don't belong to them.

Ever heard of Artificial Intelligence, or AI for short? It's this really cool technology that lets computers think and learn like humans. Imagine robots that can play games, answer questions, or even draw pictures! But, just like a coin has two sides, AI can also get a bit tricky. While it can do awesome stuff, we also need to be careful because sometimes AI can make mistakes, like mixing up facts or creating things that aren't true if it's not taught the right way. It's super important to keep our personal stuff safe from these AI tricks.

Fake Images and Deepfakes: AI can make fake pictures that look real! It's super important to check where the image comes from before believing it.

Fake Social Media Accounts: AI can create fake people online! Not everyone you talk to is who they say they are.

AI "Fake Friends" and Manipulation: Older people and criminals can use AI to make fake friends that try to trick you into giving away your personal info, harming yourself, or harming other people! Don't talk to strangers online!

Impersonating Voices: AI can copy voices and make it sound like someone you know! Always be careful who you listen to online.

AI's Trickery with Videos and Audio: AI can create fake videos or audios of people saying things they never actually did or said. They sound real, even though they're fake! Always question what you see and hear.

AI-Generated Fake News: AI can create false headlines or news stories, tricking people into believing things that aren't true.

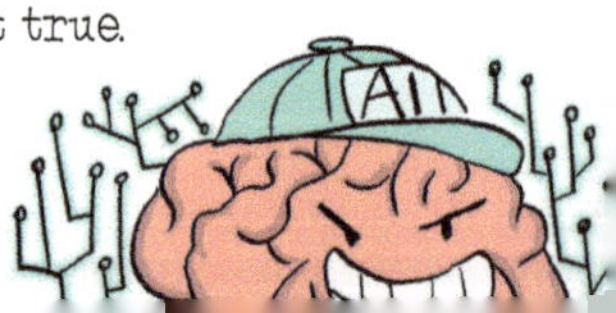

Mia, Max, and the Great Freebie Frenzy!

1: The Digital Rollercoaster Begins

2: Ad Attack Avalanche

3: The Data Grabbing Grabber Machine

4: The Privacy Pirates

5: The Cookie Monster Trap

6: The End of the Ride – The Realization

7: The Wise Decision

"Remember, Tiny Tycoons, in the digital world, free rides might cost more than you think! Stay smart, stay safe!"

Smart Moves in the Freebie Jungle

1. Ad Detective: We learned to spot ads and not get hypnotized by them.
2. Time Check: We also decided not to get sucked into the freebie vortex for too long. There's a whole world outside waiting for us!

The Real Deal About Free Stuff

- **Ad Attack:** Ever notice how free games are ad-magnets? Yeah, that's the deal. Ads are like the rent we pay for playing. Do not click, or you'll get sucked into a not-so-fun vortex!

- **Info Watch:** Remember, some apps are like info-collectors. It's cool when they make games better, but sharing your info? Hmm, think twice.

Why You Should Care

- **Privacy is King (or Queen):** Your info is precious. Keep it locked up like a crown jewel.

- **Smart Choices Rock:** Knowing the truth behind free stuff helps you become a digital genius, picking what's good for you and how much time you spend.

Stay Sharp and Safe

1. **Question Everything:** See a free app? Ask yourself, why's it free? What kind of ads do I see? Do I feel comfortable with this?

2. **Adults to the Rescue:** Always chat with your folks about the apps you're into. They're like your co-pilots in navigating the digital skies.

3. **Time Treasure:** Even if it's free, remember, your time's worth more than gold. Don't let an app turn you into a screen zombie or take you away from other fun or important activities.

Quiz Time: The Wise User Challenge

Pick a free app you like and play detective. Why's it free? What's the deal with its ads or how it handles your info?

POP QUIZ!

Put on your detective hats and uncover the secrets behind your favourite free apps and games? Let's dive in! >>>

1. Pick a Free App or Game You Use Often:

Write down the name of the app/game.

2. Why Do You Think It's Free?

A) The app shows a lot of ads.
B) It's just really nice of the developers to make it free.
C) The app offers in-app purchases.
D) I'm not sure.

3. Have You Noticed Ads While Using It?

A) Yes, they pop up quite often.
B) Only a few, not too annoying.
C) No, I haven't seen any ads.
D) Not sure, I don't pay attention to them.

4. What Kind of Ads Do You Usually See?

A) Ads that seem to know what I like.
B) Ads about toys, snacks, or clothes.
C) Ads related to other games or apps.
D) I'm not sure/I don't remember.

5. Does the App Ask for Permissions or Information About You?

A) Yes, it asks for access to my contacts, photos, or location.
B) No, it doesn't ask for any personal information.
C) It asks for some information, but I don't think it's too personal.
D) I'm not sure what it asks for.

6. What Would You Do If an App Asks to Track Your Phone?

A) Say yes, because more features are always better.
B) Say no, because I like keeping my adventures private.
C) Ignore it. If I don't see it, it's not there, right?
D) Ask a grown-up what it means before deciding.

7. Why Do You Think the App/Game Collects Data About Your Usage?

A) To sell the data to other companies.
B) To make the app/game better and more fun for me.
C) To show me ads that match my interests.
D) I never thought about it.

8. Have You Ever Made an In-App Purchase?

A) Yes, I've bought things a few times.
B) No, I use it completely for free.
C) Once or twice, just to try it.
D) I'm not allowed to make in-app purchases.

Reflection Time!

Check out your answers. Picked lots of As and Cs? Then your go-to free app might be mixing fun with sneaky ad tricks or peeking into your game time for cash. Yep, while you're in game-land, they're making bank! Knowing why an app is on the house makes you a smart gamer. Loving free apps is cool, but spotting the catch? That's being a real Wise User.

You've played detective, now let's crack the code on those sneaky ads!

Signs of a Sneaky Ad:

- An ad promising unlimited game coins for free (too good to be true).

- Another asking for an email or phone number to claim a prize (personal info alert).

"This adventure has taught us a lot about the digital world," said Max. "And how to enjoy it without giving away too much of ourselves," added Mia.

Wrapping up, Tiny Tycoons, remember the digital world's full of 'free' surprises, but not all are what they seem. Being smart and cautious makes you not just a user, but a digital trailblazer. Share this secret with your pals, and let's make the digital world a better, safer playground!

Update patch complete,
Mia & Max (currently trying to decode whether an image is real or not – it's like a puzzle, but less fun).

Chapter 5: Dopamine Dilemma - The Battle of Brains and Screens

Update Patch #5: The Great Dopamine Adventure

Hey there, Brainy Bunch! It's Mia and Max, back with a super-secret mission – decoding the mysterious world of dopamine. You know, that tiny superhero in your brain that loves to have fun? Well, it's time to learn about its tricks and treats!

Dopamine: The Brain's Own not-so-Superhero

Imagine dopamine as a tiny superhero inside your brain, flying around with a cape, giving high-fives when you feel happy or excited. It loves everything from scoring goals in soccer to acing a test. But guess what? It also goes bananas over likes on social media and winning in video games!

The Double-Edged Sword of Digital Fun

Here's where it gets tricky. Apps and games are like dopamine candy stores. They're designed to make your brain's superhero jump with joy. Every swipe, like, or level-up is like a dopamine donut – super tasty but not always good in large amounts.

Have you ever found yourself scrolling, scrolling, and just... still scrolling on social media? That's the dopamine superhero having a never-ending party. But, too much partying, and it forgets about other cool stuff like building a spaceship from LEGO or drawing your comic book.

Most games are like a playground for our dopamine superhero, with rewards, adventure, bright colours and fun victory sounds. It's like being at an amusement park where the rides never stop. Super fun, yes, but even superheroes need a break!

Here's the secret: companies know all about our dopamine superhero. They create these attractive apps and games that keep dopamine so busy partying that it forgets the time. It's like a magician using a distraction so you don't see the rabbit popping out of the hat.

The Savvy Young Creator's Guide to Dopamine

1. **The Balance Beam:** Imagine walking on a beam – too much to one side, and whoops, you might fall! Balance your screen time with other superhero activities like sports, art, or reading.

2. **Time Treasure Chest:** Set a timer when you're watching TV, using apps or playing games. When the time's up, it's your cue to do something else awesome.

3. **The Power of Pause:** Learn to press the pause button. Feel like you're in a never-ending scroll? Take a deep breath, and switch to doing something that involves no screens.

- **Spot the Tricks:** Remember, every app or game is like a magician's show. Enjoy the magic but watch out for the tricks.

- **Be a Creator, Not Just a Consumer:** Instead of scrolling or playing endlessly, think about what cool things you can create. Maybe design your own game or start a fun project.

- **The Goldfish Challenge:** Ever watched a goldfish in a bowl? It swims round and round, kind of like endless scrolling. Don't be the goldfish! Swim out of the bowl and explore the ocean.

- **Be the Boss of Your Time:** Decide how long you'll spend on screens. It's like being the captain of a ship – you decide the route and when to dock.

- **Your Time, Your Treasure:** Remember, your time is a treasure chest. Don't spend it all making someone else rich by playing their games. Use it to build your own dreams and talents.

Don't forget, like too much of any good thing, there's a flip side to Dopamine. Dopamine's thrill from endless games and scrolls can lead us to miss out on epic real-life adventures. Imagine skipping a real treasure hunt because you're glued to collecting digital coins. Or forgetting to laugh with friends because you're counting likes. When dopamine keeps us locked to screens, we miss the awesome stuff beyond – like creating a masterpiece or scoring a real goal under the sun. It's about balancing the superhero's powers with the whole universe of fun waiting outside the digital world.

Conclusion: The Master of Your Brain's Superhero

So, as we end this mission, remember you're the boss of your brain's superhero. Keep it busy with fun, learning, and creativity. And hey, sometimes, let it enjoy a little screen time – but remember to take breaks and try other fun activities!

Update patch complete
Signing off with superhero capes,
Ellie, Mia & Max (currently designing our own superhero capes – because why not?).

What would your cape look like?

Draw it here:

AWESOME!!

Chapter 6: Balance in the Digital Playground (Healthy Digital Habits)

Update Patch #6: Finding Harmony in a Digital World

Hey there, Digital Explorers! Ellie here, zipping through cyberspace with Mia and Max, who are currently on a mission to beat their high score in 'Garden Defender' (it's getting intense). But pause that game, because we've got a new quest: navigating the digital world with balance. Think of it like levelling up in real life, where the game is all about mixing screen time with sun time. So, controllers down, adventurers – let's find that perfect balance and power up our real-world skills!

We love exploring the digital playground, but we also knew it was important to find balance. One sunny day, we decided to plan how we could enjoy our digital activities while also making time for other important things in our lives.

Ellie the explorer joined us with her notebook, and together, we came up with the idea of a 'Digital Diet' - balancing our time online with other activities. **"Just like we balance our food with fruits, veggies, and treats, we can balance our digital activities too,"** said Ellie.

Creating a Balanced Schedule

1. **Set Time Limits:** We decided to spend no more than an hour at a time on our devices. After that, we would take a break and do something else.

2. **Diverse Activities:** We made a list that included playing outside, reading, crafting, and spending time with family. **"Mia loves drawing, while Max enjoys building models"**, Ellie wrote in her notebook.

We agreed on 'digital time-outs' – periods when we would put away all digital devices. During meals, family gatherings, and before bedtime were chosen as device-free times.

We also decided to spend time learning new skills that didn't involve screens. **"Today, Mia started gardening, and Max began learning to play the guitar, whilst I learnt the important skill of map reading and navigating the great outdoors with their dad"**, Ellie wrote again in her notebook.

After Ellie went home, our parents helped by setting up parental controls on our devices to encourage outdoor activities. We also spent time together as a family without any screens, chatting about our day and playing board games. We learnt some really cool stuff from mum and dad like the epic water balloon fight dad organized in his neighbourhood as a child and the time mum built a treehouse using only recycled materials with the help of grandpa and grandma. They even shared about mum's adventure of accidentally turning the office meeting into a virtual dance party because of a mistaken screen share! These stories not only made us laugh but showed us how creativity and fun don't just belong to kids.

We learnt about trust and now know that if anyone online tries to get us to hide something from our parents or forces us to keep secrets, then we must definitely report this to our parents. It's like when you are part of a team in a game of hide and seek. If someone from the opposite team tries to convince you to give away your teammates' hiding spots, you know it's against the rules and the spirit of the game. Just like in the game, if someone online is asking you to keep secrets from your parents, they're trying to trick you into breaking the trust of your most important team - your family. So, just as you would in the game, it's best to stick to the rules and tell your parents.

We also talked about choosing digital content wisely with mum and dad. We opted for educational TV shows, games and apps that encouraged learning and creativity.

Digital Diet Choices

At the end of each week, we reflected on our digital use, discussing what we enjoyed and what we could change for the next week.

The digital world, like a giant playground, is full of fun and interesting things. But spending too much time there can make us miss out on other great experiences in life, like playing outside, reading books, or spending time with family and friends.

Building Healthy Digital Habits

1. **Set Time Limits:** Like deciding how long you'll stay at a party, set a time limit for how long you'll use digital devices. It helps you enjoy other activities too.

2. **Take Regular Breaks:** Just like taking a breather after running around, take breaks from screen time. Rest your eyes and stretch your body.

3. **Be Active:** Make sure you move and play, not just sit and stare. Active games, sports, and outdoor adventures are important for your health.

4. **Tech-Free Zones:** Create special areas at home where no digital devices are allowed, like the dining room during meals. This helps in enjoying time with family.

A Day in a Balanced Digital Life

MORNING: Start with a fun outdoor activity like running or a creative project.

AFTERNOON: Spend some time on educational apps or games.

EVENING: Read a book or play a board game with family. No screens before bed to help you sleep better.

Your Digital Diet

Just like eating fruits, veggies, and treats in the right amounts, balance your 'digital diet.' Mix learning apps, creative tools, and fun games in healthy proportions.

Challenge: Create Your Balanced Day

Plan Your Day: Make a schedule that includes digital activities, outdoor play, creative time, and family time. Share it with your family and try it out!

Staying Balanced is Fun!

The digital world is like a giant candy store – super cool and full of treats, but you wouldn't want candy for breakfast, lunch, and dinner, right? Mia and I figured out that mixing up our fun, like a great adventure playlist, made everything way more awesome. We cooked up a 'Digital Diet' that's part online exploration, part real-world discovery, and shared it with all our friends. It's all about hitting that sweet spot between screen time and sun time!

Chapter 7: Young Innovators in Action (Real Stories)

Update Patch #7: The Young Genius Showcase

Hey, future world-changers! It's Mia and Max here with your ticket to the Hall of Young Innovators – kids who turned "maybe someday" into "look at me now!"

Armed with our tablets (and a strict one-hour timer, because balance), we journeyed into the world of kid geniuses. From tech wizards to eco-warriors, these kids are redefining cool.

Marley Dias:
The Literary Game-Changer

Marley Dias, only 11, and already a hero in the book world. She launched #1000BlackGirlBooks to bring diversity to her school library. Now she's a voice for change and even penned her own book!

Namya Joshi:
Minecraft Educator

Namya Joshi, 13, transformed school lessons into Minecraft adventures. She's proof that games and learning are a match made in heaven.

Gitanjali Rao:

Science Prodigy

Meet Gitanjali Rao, the 11-year-old who tackled the Flint water crisis with "Tethys," a lead detection tool. She's America's Top Young Scientist and a beacon of hope for a better world.

Hekma Jabouli:

Revolutionizing Healthcare with Innovation

Revolutionizing Healthcare with Innovation-Hekma Jabouli: From Syria, Hekma's smart device is helping her sister walk again – an innovation born from love and necessity.

Thomas Suarez:
A Young App Developer

This app-developing whiz kid started at 9 and founded CarrotCorp by 12. He's not just coding apps; he's shaping futures.

Vinusha MK:
The Young Chef and Entrepreneur

A 10-year-old baking entrepreneur from India, her Four Seasons Pastry is a sweet blend of culinary art and business savvy.

John Wobil:

Pioneering Agricultural Advances

Hailing from Ghana, his innovative rice thresher is revolutionizing agriculture, one grain at a time.

Edwin Inganji:

Enhancing Safety through Technology

After surviving an assault, Edwin created Usalama in Kenya, a distress signal app that's all about safety first.

James Van der Walt:

Lighting Up Lives with Solar Power

In South Africa, his 'Solar Turtle' is bringing power to off-grid communities, proving that great ideas shine bright.

Alex Makalliwa:

Electrifying Transportation Solutions

He's driving change in Nairobi with electric tuk-tuks and solar charging, steering towards a sustainable future.

Rayna Singh:

Empowering Girls Through Self-Defence

At 17, she's empowering girls in Delhi's slums with self-defence skills, proving courage knows no age.

Ananya Kamboj:

Using Sports for Gender Equality

Using sports as her platform, she's a voice for gender equality, showing that change can start with a game.

Wall of Inspiration: A Daily Dose of Awesome

We shared these incredible stories at school, and with Mr. Eaton's help, created a 'Wall of Inspiration.' It's our daily reminder that age is just a number when it comes to making a difference.

These young heroes show that your ideas can light up the world. Dream it, plan it, make it happen. You're never too young to be an innovator.

Challenge: Innovator's Log

Start an Innovator's Log. Jot down your wild, wacky, wonderful ideas. Sketch, plan, dream. Who knows? You might just be the next name on our Wall of Inspiration!

Remember, every giant leap starts with a small step. You've got the power to innovate, create, and inspire. So go ahead, be the story that sparks a million more!

Logbook out,
Mia & Max (currently brainstorming our next big project – it's going to be out of this world!).

Chapter 8: Your Creator's Journey (Getting Started)

Update Patch #8: Launching Your Creator Quest

Hey, Creative Commanders! It's Max and Mia here, ready to guide you on the most epic adventure yet – your very own creator's journey. It's like unlocking a new level in the coolest game ever!

Mia & Max's Blueprint to Becoming Makers

After marvelling at those young geniuses, we were itching to start our own projects. Here's how we kicked off our creator's journey, and you can too!

Step 1: Passion Patrol

- **Activity:** Brainstorm what gets your gears grinding. Is it robots, rockets, or recreating the Taj Mahal in LEGO?

- **Purpose:** Pinpointing your passions is like finding your superpower. It's where the magic begins!

Step 2: Mini-Mission Launch

- **Activity:** Pick an easy-peasy project. Draw your dream treehouse or code a simple game.

- **Purpose:** Small wins = big grins. It's all about building confidence one tiny victory at a time.

Step 3: Treasure Hunt for Tools

- **Activity:** Scavenge for resources. Old magazines, online tutorials, or a pile of recyclables can be your goldmine.

- **Purpose:** Resourcefulness is a creator's best friend. Plus, it's eco-friendly and wallet-happy!

Step 4: Creation Station

- **Activity:** Dive into your project. Embrace the mess-ups – they're just plot twists in your inventor's tale.

- **Purpose:** Hands-on doing is the best kind of learning. Plus, who doesn't like a good challenge?

Step 5: Feedback Fiesta

- **Activity:** Show off your creation to your fan club (aka family and friends). Enjoy the cheers and take in helpful tips to make your creation even better.

- **Purpose:** Feedback is like a special boost in your creative journey. It helps you see what's awesome and what you can improve!

Step 6: Sharing is Daring

- **Activity:** Share your masterpiece in class, at a community show, or even online (grown-up-approved, of course).

- **Purpose:** Sharing your work with others spreads creativity and might inspire them to create their own masterpieces!

Step 7: Reflect and Rocket Forward

- **Activity:** After your project, take a moment to reflect. What rocked? What could be even rockier?

- **Purpose:** Reflection is your roadmap. It shows where you've been and where you're headed next.

1: Digital Creation Challenge Announcement

2: Kids Starting Digital Projects

3: Overcoming Digital Challenges

4: Collaborative Online Interaction

5: Showcasing Digital Creations

6: Celebrating Digital Creativity

Discovering Your Creative Compass

- **Explore Your World:** Your interests are like stars guiding your journey. Follow them to find your creative constellation.

- **Knowledge Quest:** Dive into books, videos, or clubs to fuel your creative engine. The more you know, the more you can create.

Kickstarting Your First Project

- **Start Simple:** Remember, Rome wasn't built in a day. Start with something small and watch it grow.

- **Use What You've Got:** Channel your inner Sherlock and use everyday stuff to build something extraordinary.

Sharing Your Creative Spark

- **Family and Friends First:** Your inner circle is your cheer squad. Show them what you've got!

- **Embrace the Good Words:** Feedback is the breakfast of champions. Eat up the good and improve on the rest.

Rising Above Roadblocks

- Mistake = Lesson: Every oops is an opportunity. Learn, laugh, and leap forward.

- Persistence Pays Off: If plan A flops, there are 25 more letters. Keep going!

HEY THERE, TINY TYCOONS!

Ready to find your crew? Join clubs or groups where ideas soar and creativity flows. Whether online or offline, choose spaces that help you grow, learn, and create—just make sure it's a safe and supportive place!

Join the Club!

Imagine a clubhouse where every idea gets quality, not mean, feedback and creativity is the secret handshake. That's the kind of club we're talking about! Look for places where you can be a super producer and creator, not just a consumer.

BUT WAIT! Here's the tricky part. If you find yourself in a club that's more about wasting time than making awesome things, or if they're into destroying stuff (like your time, your cool gadgets, or even your good vibes), then sound the alarm! You should never do things to harm yourself or other people, even if it's meant to be **"just for fun"**. That club is a no-go zone.

Every club, community, or digital hangout spot you join should get the thumbs-up from your biggest fans – your parents. But hey, remember, even parents can miss a trick sometimes.
So, you got the green light from your folks and joined a club, but uh-oh, something feels off? If you spot any not-so-cool activities or things that make you go **"Hmm..."**, it's time for a parent-kid huddle. Get your parents to take a second look and reassess. Safety first, fun second!

One time, Max and I were super excited to join 'The Legendary Crafters,' a club we found online. It promised endless crafting adventures. After getting a thumbs-up from mum and dad, we dove in. But soon, we noticed the projects involved a lot of pranks, using stuff around the house in ways we weren't supposed to. Something felt icky about turning mum's favourite vase into a homemade volcano without her permission. We called a family meeting, showed our parents the club activities, and together, we decided it was time to find a new adventure. This club wasn't about creating joy, but mischief that could hurt feelings or break trust. Lesson learned: when in doubt, check it out (with mum and dad)

Your Club, Your Rules

Find a place that makes you excited to create, learn, and share. A club where you're the hero of your own story, not just a side character in someone else's game. Remember, the best clubs make you feel like you're soaring, not snoring!

So gear up, Tiny Tycoons, and find your tribe where you can shine bright, create wonders, and maybe even change the world!

Show Off Your Stuff:

Competitions and exhibitions aren't just about winning – they're about giving things a go and boosting your confidence.

It's time to step into the spotlight and show the world what you've got. But here's a little secret: the best stages are the ones where you can truly sparkle with your talent and skills.

Get your behind-the-scenes heroes (yep, your parents!) to scout out the coolest competitions and exhibitions for you. Be on the lookout for places where your creativity can shine, not just where you do the latest dance moves or wacky challenges – unless of course your super power is dancing!

Say 'No' to Silly Show-Offs

And listen up, champions! Not all challenges are worth your time, especially not those Tik-Tok types that ask you to do stuff that's, well, a bit bonkers (and not in the good way). Remember, you're not just there to be the entertainment or the laugh of the day.

YOU'RE A TiNY TYCOON!

You're the Star, Not the Product

When you pick the right stage – be it a science fair, an art exhibition, or a coding contest – you're showing off your hardwork and skills. That's where you're the main event, not just part of the sideshow. Let's skip the goofy stuff and go for the glory where you add real sparkle to the world! Have fun in a way that makes you feel comfortable, not just because other people are doing it.

So, put on those thinking caps, grab your tools of the trade, and let's find the perfect stage for you to shine and share. Because in the right light, you're not just a star –

YOU'RE A SUPERNOVA!

Dreaming and Doing

- **Aim for the Stars:** What's your big dream? Invent something life-changing? Start your own business? Go for it!

- **Plan It to Nail It:** Dreams without plans are just wishes. Unless you're a genie, you can't sit back and rub your wishes to life – you need to get moving, get doing Chart your course and set sail!

Remember, fellow Tiny Tycoons, being a creator is about exploring, expressing, and making the world a bit more awesome. Your journey starts now. Who knows where your ideas will take you? The most important part? Enjoy the ride and keep on creating!

Max and Mia signing off (currently brainstorming our next wild invention – it involves a cat, a drone, and a whole lot of duct tape. Stay tuned!).

F
U
T
U
R
E

Conclusion: The Future is Yours to Create

Update Patch #9: The Grand Finale - Your Future Awaits!

Hello, Future World Shapers! Max and Mia here, signing off from our Tycoon Town adventure. But guess what? This isn't "The End." Nope, it's just the very beginning of something even more awesome – your story.

The world's like a giant canvas, and you've got the coolest set of colors (your ideas, dreams, and talents) to paint it. Think of Mia and Max's escapades as just a warm-up. Now, it's your turn to grab the brush!

From the tales of young innovators to our own little adventures, one thing's crystal clear – no matter your size, your age, or where you come from, you can make waves. Big ideas don't always come from big people; sometimes, the smallest people have the mightiest dreams. I know we say "Tiny Tycoons" but there sure is nothing tiny about that mind of yours!

Being a creator is more than just making stuff. It's about constantly learning, adapting, and growing. Got a hiccup in your project? That's not failure; that's just life giving you extra homework. Every stumble is a new lesson. And hey, lessons are cool.

You've got the superpowers – to create, to choose wisely, and to keep yourself from becoming just a cog in the digital machine. You're not just playing the game; you're designing it, leveling up in real life.

Your brain is a storm of brilliant ideas. You could be the next great inventor, artist, scientist, or leader. The world's a puzzle waiting for you to solve, a song waiting for you to write, a canvas waiting for your brush.

Remember, every big castle was built one brick at a time. If your first plan doesn't work out, don't worry, just try again and make it better. The journey to greatness is all about taking those baby steps, and then one day, you'll look back and see how far you've come.

Stay curious. Ask questions, explore, and discover new things every day. The more you learn, the more you can do. And remember, knowing what you don't know is a superpower too. It helps you keep growing and collaborating.

Share your journey, your learnings, and even your goof-ups. Because when we share, we grow. Lighting up someone else's path doesn't dim your own; it makes the world brighter.

The future? It's like an unwritten book, and you're the author. So, write a good one. With every new sunrise, you've got a chance to sketch, to build, to play, and to change the game.

As we end our Tycoon Town: CyberMental adventure, remember, your story is just getting started. The world's waiting for your mark – your creations, your ideas, and your dreams. Dream big, create bigger, and never stop turning the pages. The future's bright, and you're the one holding the flashlight, so enjoy the journey.

So long, Tiny Tycoons, but not goodbye. The future's yours to create, and we can't wait to see what you make of it!

Logbook out,
Mia & Max **(off to our next adventure, and we'll be keeping an eye out for your epic stories in the making!).**

Bye etc!

More Cool Kids to Inspire You

GUESS WHAT? The adventure's not over! Mia, Max, and I found a whole bunch more brainy buddies who've turned their big dreams into super cool realities. They're just like us, Tiny Tycoons in the making, who chose to do something awesome. Ready for more wow-worthy stories? Dive into this bonus round of young creators who are shaping our world!

Mikaila Ulmer: Mikaila started her own lemonade business at the age of 4 and later founded "Me & the Bees Lemonade" at the age of 11. Her company promotes sustainable practices and donates a portion of its profits to organizations working to save honeybees.

Elif Bilgin: At just 4, Elif from Turkey taught herself to read and write and started her inventing journey at 8. Inspired at 14 to tackle plastic pollution in Istanbul's waters, she innovatively created bioplastic from banana peels. Her successful experiment earned her awards like the Google Science Fair 2013 and Voters' Choice Awards. She later pursued biomedical engineering and computer science and landed a job at Google as a software engineer.

Braeden Mannering: At the age of 9, Braeden founded "Brae's Brown Bags" to provide healthy food to homeless and low-income individuals. His initiative has made a significant impact in his community and beyond.

Noa Mintz: Noa started a babysitting business at the age of 12, which later became "Nannies by Noa," handling over 190 clients. She handed over control to a full-time CEO upon entering high school due to the business's growth.

Jason Li: At the age of 15, Jason founded iReTron, an electronics refurbishment company, with a $2,000 loan from his father. The company buys old electronics, refurbishes them, and sells them for a profit

Shroff: Featured as the youngest innovator on a list of 16 innovators to watch in 2022, Shroff is working on improving her A.I. model by adding millions of wildfire data points. She is also collaborating with researchers at Arizona State University to develop a drone deployment for spraying flame retardant, with the aim of combating wildfires.

Mikey Wren: Mikey teaches financial literacy to kids in his community and has written two books on the subject, demonstrating a strong entrepreneurial spirit at a young age.

Aline Morse, Hannah Grace, and Maddie Rae: These young entrepreneurs founded Zolli Candy, BeYOUtiful, and Maddie Rae's Slime Glue, respectively, showcasing the diverse range of businesses started by young individuals.

Ranveer Sandhu: At 17 years old, Sandhu gained over 5 years of experience in the property industry and personal development, exemplifying the early expertise and entrepreneurship of young individuals.

Hannah Herbst: Introduced to engineering at a summer camp, Hannah Herbst, the only girl there, was inspired by her pen pal in Sub-Saharan Africa to create BEACON—a device harnessing ocean wave energy for developing countries. Her innovative work earned her the 2015 Discovery Education 3M Young Scientist Challenge title, recognition at the United Nations, and numerous awards, showcasing her world-changing efforts.

Rifath Shaarook: Rifath Shaarook's innovation is truly out of this world! He was able to develop KalamSat, the world's lightest satellite from scratch! Although this was not his first invention, the Indian innovator created a cube-sized, lightweight satellite that weighs in at 0.14 pounds! KalamSat was launched into space by NASA in June 2017 and was carried by the Terrier Orion rocket. Rifath's work will help lead to smaller and more cost-efficient and eco-friendly satellites!

Erin Smith: While still in high school, Erin Smith developed Faceprint, an innovative tool using facial recognition technology for early detection of Parkinson's Disease and other neurological disorders. Inspired by a Michael J. Fox Foundation video, she observed distant emotions in smiles and laughs as early signs. Erin aims to revolutionize disease detection and treatment with her life-saving work.

Fionn Ferreira: 20-year-old Irish inventor and environmentalist Fionn Ferreira, inspired by his seaside upbringing, developed devices to detect and extract microplastics from water sustainably. His groundbreaking work won him the 2019 Google Science Fair, leading him to establish Fionn & Co., aiming to scale up his inventions for broader environmental impact.

Xóchitl Guadalupe Cruz López: At just 11 years old, Xóchitl from Mexico innovated the "Warm Bath," a solar-powered water heater using recycled materials to provide accessible hot water for low-income communities and reduce deforestation. This creation, earning her a prestigious science prize from Mexico's UNAM at 9, represents a significant win for both people and the environment.

Doris Sung: Doris Sung is working on designing energy-saving windows. Her innovative designs aim to contribute to energy efficiency in buildings, addressing a significant aspect of environmental sustainability.

Toby Kiers and Colin Averill: These innovators are focused on mapping fungi and their beneficial relationship with plant species. Their work has the potential to impact agricultural practices and ecosystem sustainability.

Eve Gregoriou: Eve is the founder of NeuroVirt. Her entrepreneurial venture is focused on utilizing her expertise in the field of neuroscience to create innovative solutions.

Unlock the Magic of New Words

As we travel through our tales and inventions, we stumble upon some pretty curious and sparkly words that might make you scratch your head and wonder, 'What in the world of Tycoon Town does that mean?'

DON'T WORRY! We've gathered all those tricky words and tucked them into this special Word Treasure Chest, just for you. Each word is like a hidden gem, and we're here to help you uncover their secrets so you can become even smarter and cooler (if that's even possible, because you're pretty awesome already!).

So, grab your explorer's hat and let's dive into this chest together. Who knows what new worlds each word will unlock? Ready, set, adventure!

Adventures: Exciting experiences or journeys. In "TiNY TYCOONS," adventures happen both in the real world and in digital playgrounds.

App: Short for application, a type of software designed to perform specific tasks or provide entertainment, accessible on digital devices like smartphones and tablets.

Artificial Intelligence (AI): Computers or machines designed to think and learn like humans. Max and Mia use AI to make their inventions smarter but are also aware that AI could be maliciously used to manipulate their personal information

Balance: Finding the right amount between different activities. It's important to balance screen time with outdoor play, reading, and spending time with family.

Bazillion: A bazillion means a very, very large number—so many that it's hard to count! It's just a fun way to say "a huge amount" of something.

Blueprint: Detailed drawings or plans that guide the creation of things like buildings, machines, or even playgrounds.

Brainstorm: When you brainstorm, you think of as many ideas as you can, no matter how silly or big they seem. It's like a thinking adventure where all your ideas come together!

Clutter: Clutter is when there's too much stuff around—things are messy and hard to find! It's like when your room is so full of toys that you can't find your favorite one.

Code/Coding: Writing instructions for computers so they can perform tasks or create games. Max loves coding new games for him and Mia to play.

Creators: People who make new things. In the story, creators use their imagination to invent, build, and create digital wonders.

CyberMental: A play on the words Cyber (all about computers, the internet, and virtual reality) and fundamental (which means super important or basic stuff we need to know). It's like saying using your electronic devices and the internet safely is the most important part of your journey as a user and a creator.

Data Privacy: The aspect of information technology that deals with the ability an organization or individual has to determine what data in a computer system can be shared with third parties.

Digital Footprint: The record or trail left by the things you do online, including websites visited, emails sent, and information submitted to online services.

Digital Playground: A space where kids can explore, learn, and have fun with technology, like coding games or creating art on a computer.

Diversity: Including a variety of different people, ideas, or things. Mia's art shows diversity with colors and themes.

Double-Edged Sword: A double-edged sword is something that can be both good and bad at the same time. Like if a game is fun, but you can spend too much time on it, forgetting about other things you need to do.

Eco-Heroes: Individuals committed to protecting the environment. They engage in activities like recycling and using eco-friendly products

Ecosystem: A community of living things and their environment. Eco-heroes protect ecosystems by recycling and saving water

Feedback: Comments or advice on how to improve something. Mia and Max learn from feedback to make their inventions even better.

Gadgets: Small electronic devices designed to serve a particular function. Max loves inventing new gadgets.

Glitch: A glitch is when something stops working right for a moment, like when your video game freezes or the screen skips. It's like a little hiccup in the system.

Imagination: The ability to think of new and creative ideas. It's your imagination that turns daydreams into real inventions or stories.

Innovation: Coming up with new ideas or ways to do things. The Tiny Tycoons are all about innovation in technology and creativity.

Interactive: Refers to technology or activities that allow for a two-way exchange of information, where users can actively participate or control the outcome.

Makers: Another word for creators, producers or inventors. Makers love to build, craft, and make new things from their ideas.

Mastermind: A mastermind is a person who comes up with a clever plan or idea, like a leader or inventor who thinks of smart ways to solve problems.

Malicious: Wanting to hurt someone or make them feel bad

Manipulate: control or influence (a person or situation) cleverly

Monetization: The process of earning revenue from an asset, product, or service. In the context of digital products, it often refers to making money through advertising, subscriptions, or selling user data.

Montage: A montage is a bunch of different things put together to show something, like when you see quick clips of someone building something or trying different ideas in a movie.

Mural: A large picture painted on a wall. Mia dreams of painting murals that inspire people.

Online Community: A group of people with common interests who use the internet to communicate, share information, and in some cases, collaborate on projects.

Pawn in Someone Else's Game: When someone else is making the decisions and using you to do what they want, instead of you being in control of your own choices.

Personal Information: Data that can be used to identify, contact, or locate a single person, or to identify an individual in context.

Pollution: Harmful substances in the air, water, or land. The Tiny Tycoons come up with ideas to reduce pollution.

Producers: People who create content or products. In "TINY TYCOONS," producers are kids who bring their creative ideas to life.

Programming Language: A formal language comprising a set of instructions used to produce various kinds of output. Programming languages are used in computer programming to implement algorithms.

Quest: A search or pursuit made in order to find or obtain something. Every new invention starts as a quest for Mia and Max.

Recycling: The process of converting waste materials into new materials and objects. It's a way to protect the environment and reduce garbage.

Scavenge: To scavenge means to look around and collect things you need, like when you find cool items outside or in a pile of things to reuse. It's like a treasure hunt!

Screen Time: The amount of time spent using a device with a screen such as a smartphone, computer, television, or video game console.

Sustainability: Using resources in a way that does not harm the environment. Mia and Max focus on sustainable projects that protect the planet

Tech-Savvy: Having practical knowledge and skills in technology, especially relating to computers and the internet.

Unscrupulous: Lacking concern for honesty, fairness.

Upcycling: Taking used or old items and making them into something new and useful. Mia and Max upcycle materials for their inventions.

Users: People who enjoy and use things that creators and producers make, like playing a game or reading a book someone else wrote.

Wisdom: Having knowledge and good judgement. Being a wise user means making smart choices about how and when to use technology.

Zany: Zany means silly, funny, or weird in a fun way. It's like when someone does something goofy, and everyone laughs because it's so unexpected and silly.

Acknowledgements

This book was born from a time of deep frustration and reflection; a time when I felt like my daughter's confidence was put to the test. As a parent, I felt powerless watching the struggle, but it reminded me of the profound impact teachers (at home and in school) can have on a child's sense of self-worth. Good teachers (like Mrs. Pickett, Mr. Eaton, Mrs Male, and Mr. Wilks) don't just teach—they help children feel confident, valued, and capable of reaching for their dreams. It was this realization that fuelled my determination to formalise my role as a teacher to my children, and hopefully to others, ensuring that they have the tools to navigate an increasingly tricky digital and physical world.

I am therefore deeply grateful to everyone who has been part of this journey. To my children—who were not only my inspiration but also my early readers, providing invaluable feedback as I worked through the story. Their journey is my own, and they will continue to be a part of this adventure, sharing videos about the book and helping it come to life in new ways. Your resilience, creativity and joy make this book shine.

I'm also thankful to the professionals who brought their expertise to this project: to Eric Smith, my developmental editor, whose insight and guidance was helpful in fine-tuning this story; to Sarah-Leigh Wills, whose illustrations brought CyberMental to life with such vibrant energy.

A heartfelt thank you to my beta readers—Dunni, Melissa, Kaylee, Marho (whom I like to call my first son) and especially Mawulom, whose support, feedback, and encouragement were essential from the start. Mawulom, you've been there since the beginning, listening to my rants, brainstorming launch ideas, and giving me that much-needed encouragement to push forward.

I am deeply grateful to my mentors, Chukwuka Akpenyi and Morenike Amiaka, whose wisdom and support have been a guiding light throughout this process, teaching me the power of balance and insight.

A heartfelt thank you to Tomi Achudume, whose unwavering emotional support has kept me grounded through the ups and downs, especially during the lowest moments of my life. To my husband, who has supported me, and will co-author the sequel MoneyMental—thank you for being my partner. Finally, to my family—my mum, mother-in-law, brother and sister—thank you for your foundational support.

"Life is in seasons, and there is a season and an appointed time for every event and purpose on earth. These were some of my dad's passing words to me the week before he died in 2024."

These words have stayed with me, reminding me that the challenges we face often have a deeper purpose, one that shapes who we are and the legacies we leave behind.

This book is a product of all your contributions, and I'm glad that the time of deep frustration has ended and the time to publish this book has come. I am forever grateful.

Also in the series

Join The Tiny Tycoons on their next adventures!

WONDERMENTAL explores how our minds work and the thinking traps we fall into, helping you explore how we think, and why we make the decisions we do.

MONEYMENTAL makes financial literacy fun through exciting challenges that teach saving, investing, and smart money choices; essential skills for a successful future!

www.thetinytycoons.com

www.ingramcontent.com/pod-product-compliance
Ingram Content Group UK Ltd.
Pitfield, Milton Keynes, MK11 3LW, UK
UKHW050149170525
458634UK00011B/35

9 781068 395703